W9-AXQ-970

TURTLE KNOWS YOUR NAME

For Jan Bradley

All Bright Wishes!

Peace
Joy

Love

Ashley Bryan

Feb 1995

TURTLE KNOWS
YOUR NAME

Retold and illustrated by

ASHLEY BRYAN

CLEARWATER PUBLIC LIBRARY SYSTEM
100 N. OSCEOLA AVE.
CLEARWATER, FL 33755

ALADDIN BOOKS
Macmillan Publishing Company   *New York*
Maxwell Macmillan Canada   *Toronto*
Maxwell Macmillan International
New York   Oxford   Singapore   Sydney

BOOKS BY ASHLEY BRYAN

The Ox of the Wonderful Horns
The Adventures of Aku
Beat the Story-Drum, Pum-Pum
Walk Together Children
I'm Going to Sing
The Dancing Granny
The Cat's Purr
Lion and the Ostrich Chicks
What a Morning!
Sh-Ko and His Eight Wicked Brothers
Turtle Knows Your Name

Retold from *Turtle Tells Her Name* (Saint Eustatius,
English Antilles). In *Folk-Lore of the Antilles,
French and English, Part II.* Elsie Clews Parsons.
New York: American Folk-Lore Society, 1936.

For JEAN KARL
If you don't mind sharing
this with another old friend,
MALCOLM FERNALD
AGE 6!

nce there was a little boy and he had a very long name.

His name was UPSILIMANA TUMPALERADO.

It was easy to pronounce, UP-SILI-MANA TUM-PA-LERADO, but it was hard to remember.

His grandmother raised him in her village by the sea.

She taught him to walk. She taught him to talk. But teaching him to walk and to talk wasn't the same as teaching him to say his name, uh-uh!

That took time, and Granny took her time. She said his name to him slowly:

"UP-SILI-MANA TUM-PA-LERADO."

"UPALA TUMPALO!" said the grandson.

"Uh-uh!" said Granny, shaking her head from side to side. "Uh-uh, uh-uh!"

She didn't give up, though.

"Turtle takes his time," she said. "I take mine, and you take your time, too."

And he did. Then one day he said it:

"UPSILIMANA TUMPALERADO!"

"Uh-huh!" cried the grandmother.

She was so happy, she hugged him once, she kissed him twice, she swung him around, wheee, three times! She shook his hand, then took his hand, and they ran down to the sandy beach.

"Here's where we dance your name dance," said Granny. "Sing your name, loud and clear. Sing it to me. Sing it to the sea!"

Granny clapped as they danced. Her grandson sang:

"UPSILIMANA TUMPALERADO,
That's my name.
I took my time to learn it,
Won't you do the same?"

Turtle, who lived nearby, heard the singing and swam closer. The villagers always came to the shore to sing and dance their children's names. Turtle loved to gather names, and he never missed a name dance. Turtle was older than anyone could tell. He even remembered Granny's name dance when Granny, as a little girl, danced with her granny on the shore. Turtle raised his head above the water and listened.

"UPSILIMANA TUMPALERADO, that's my name," sang the boy again and again.

"A long name," said Turtle. "But a good song name to dance to. I think I've got it."

Turtle flipped and dove to the bottom of the sea. In his coral home, Turtle smoothed a space and spelled the name with shells. He blinked and said:

"UPSILIMANA TUMPALERADO, uh-huh! I know it well."

Now that her grandson knew it well, too, Granny let him go out alone to play in the village. Each time he set out to play, she'd say:

"UPSILIMANA TUMPALERADO, teach your name to your playmates and do your best. Remember, your name is long, but it's not the longest."

UPSILIMANA TUMPALERADO always had a good time playing with the village children. He learned their names quickly: Zamba, Mogans, Dandoo, Brashee...and he remembered them. He taught them his name, too. But no one ever remembered it.

"Ho, Long Name!" they'd call. "Your turn to hide the stick."

"My name is not Long Name," he'd say. "My name is UPSILIMANA TUMPALERADO."

"Uh-huh," they'd say. "But it's still your turn, Long Name."

His name *was* always the longest. What, then, did Granny mean when she'd say, "Your name is long, but it's not the longest"?

One morning UPSILIMANA TUMPALERADO said, "Granny, I'm not going to be called Long Name today. I'm going to play with the animals."

"Don't be late for dinner," said Granny. "I'm cooking fungi."

"Fungi!" exclaimed the boy.

"Uh-huh!" said Granny. "If you're late, I might be tempted to eat all the fungi myself."

"Uh-uh!" said the boy. "I won't be late! You'll see. Bye, Granny. Twee-twaa-twee."

Off he went, whistling twee-twaa-twee, twee-twaa-twee.

He came to a field and saw a donkey rubbing its hide against a tree. The boy sang:

> *"Donkey, hee, donkey, oh!*
> *My name is UPSILIMANA TUMPALERADO.*
> *Shall I call it out once more?"*

The donkey brayed, "Haw, hee-haw," and rubbed its hide just as before.

"Well, twee-twaa-twee," whistled the boy, and he ran across the field. He clambered up on the rocks bordering the field. There he met a goat bounding from stone to stone. The boy sang:

> *"Goat, hah, goat, oh!*
> *My name is UPSILIMANA TUMPALERADO.*
> *Say it loud. Say it clear."*

The goat bleated, "Bleah, bleah-bleah," and leaped as if it didn't care.

"Well, twee-twaa-twee," whistled the boy. He jumped from the rocks into the pasture near the seashore. There he saw a cow. The boy sang:

> *"Cow, ho, cow, oh!*
> *My name is UPSILIMANA TUMPALERADO.*
> *Say it, and I'll dance for you."*

The cow lowed, "Moo, moo-moo," then mooed once more and stopped to chew.

"Well, twee-twaa-twee," whistled the boy. He spun around swiftly and bumped into a pig.

"Oh, pardon, pig," he said. "My name is…" and he stopped short.

"Uh-uh! I won't tell you my name. You'll do the same as the others."

He ran past pig in the pasture, past pawpaw and palm trees till he came to the beach.

He splashed in the sea, whistling, "Twee-twaa-twee."

Turtle heard the splashing. He swam up to the boy and said:

> *"UPSILIMANA TUMPALERADO,*
> *I'm so glad you came.*
> *UPSILIMANA TUMPALERADO,*
> *Turtle knows your name."*

The boy slapped the water for joy, splish-splash, splish-splash!

"Turtle, oh, Turtle," he cried. "How did you know that my name is UPSILIMANA TUMPALERADO?"

Turtle didn't stay to play or answer questions. He dove under the waves and disappeared.

The boy called and called till his stomach ached, but Turtle did not return.

"I've yelled myself hoarse, hollow, and hungry," he said to himself. "The fungi, oh, the fungi!"

He ran as fast as he could go. He ran past pawpaw and palm trees, past pig in the pasture, past cow who gazed, grazed, and mooed, past goat bounding high over the rocks, bleah-bleah, past donkey in the field, hee-haw, hee-haw. He ran into his house, crying:

"Granny! Granny! Please, I'm hungry. The fungi, the fungi!"

With her large wooden spoon, Granny was turning the cornmeal in the pot. She smiled at her grandson as she ladled some into a buttered bowl and shook it till it was round as a grapefruit. She rolled it onto her grandson's plate of fish.

"Thank you, Granny. Fungi rolled in a bowl till it's round as a ball and as yellow as gold is the best of all."

"Sing it!" said Granny. She hummed as she shook a bowl of fungi for herself:

"Fungi rolled in a bowl
Till it's round as a ball
And as yellow as gold
Is the best of all."

They finished eating the fungi and fish. Then Granny set a plate of bread pudding and a sweet-potato pie on the table.

"He who asks, don't get. He who don't ask, don't want," said Granny.

Granny always said that before offering dessert. She'd laugh as she watched the puzzled look on her grandson's face. Then she'd offer him a way out.

"Tell me a proverb," she'd say, "and I'll give you dessert."

"A proverb? No problem!" UPSILIMANA TUMPALERADO would say. He had learned lots of proverbs.

He'd answer with: "A man can't grow taller than his head" or "You'll never catch a black cat at night." His favorite was "If a baboon wants to whistle, don't stop him."

But this time, Granny didn't ask for a proverb.

Instead she said, "Tell me my name, UPSILIMANA TUMPALERADO."

"Oh, Granny, that's easier than a proverb," said the boy. "Your name is Granny!"

He laughed and passed his plate.

"Uh-uh," said Granny. "There are grannies all over the village. Every granny has a name. Tell me mine, or no dessert."

Granny took a bite of her bread pudding. UPSILIMANA TUMPALERADO looked at Granny. She licked her lips and rolled her eyes. He looked longingly at the dessert.

"I will find out your real name, Granny," he said. "Then I will have dessert, too."

UPSILIMANA TUMPALERADO jumped up from the table and ran off to the village. He stopped the villagers and asked:

"Do you know my granny's name?
Will you tell it to me plain?
I won't get bread pudding
Or sweet-potato pie
Until I tell her real name to her;
Saying 'Granny' just won't do her."

The villagers circled him and sang:

"Grass, plants, bees, bells,
Sky, birds, seas, shells,
Guava, plantain, mango trees—
Call them anything you please.
They will always be the same
'Cause Granny is your granny's name."

The villagers danced as they sang the song over and over. Drummers picked up the beat. For a while, UPSILIMANA TUMPALERADO forgot his question and danced quick steps to match the best of the dancers. Then he remembered.

"This won't get me dessert," he said to himself.

He could hear the villagers still chanting, "Granny is your granny's name," as he hurried away to the animals.

He ran to the donkey, haw, hee-haw. Donkey wouldn't help him, didn't want to. Goat and cow were just the same, wouldn't help him with the name, bleah-bleah, moo-moo.

Perhaps Turtle would help. Turtle knew his name. Turtle had said his name before. He kept on running till he reached the shore.

He called till turtle swam up from his coral home at the bottom of the sea. Then the boy sang:

"Turtle, tell me Granny's name.
Will you tell it to me plain?
I won't get bread pudding
Or sweet-potato pie
Until I tell her real name to her;
Saying 'Granny' just won't do her."

Turtle listened to the sweet, sad song. Then Turtle sang:

"UPSILIMANA TUMPALERADO,
Turtle knows your name.
Gathering names is what I do.
I know Granny's real name, too."

"Oh, teach me, Turtle, teach me!" cried the boy.

"First, promise not to tell who told you," said Turtle.

The boy promised and Turtle taught him his granny's name.

"Uh-huh! So that's why Granny always says to me, 'Your name is long, but it's not the longest.'"

He thanked Turtle and ran home.

"Dessert, please, dessert!" cried the boy as he ran into the room.

"Well, UPSILIMANA TUMPALERADO, first tell me my real name."

"Your name is MAPASEEDO JACKALINDY EYE PIE TACKARINDY!"

"Why, UPSILIMANA TUMPALERADO, that's right, uh-huh!"

She served her grandson a large square of bread pudding.

"Tell me, UPSILIMANA TUMPALERADO, who told you my name?"

"Oh, MAPASEEDO JACKALINDY EYE PIE TACKARINDY, I can't tell you."

"Why can't you tell me, UPSILIMANA TUMPALERADO?"

"I promised not to, MAPASEEDO JACKALINDY EYE PIE TACKARINDY."

"Well, then, UPSILIMANA TUMPALERADO, I'll find out for myself."

Granny put on her large straw hat and went into the village. She stopped in the marketplace and said to the villagers:

"My grandson came
And asked my name.
Did you tell it?
Who can spell it?"

The villagers clapped and sang:

> *"Long Name came*
> *And asked your name.*
> *So we told him, and it's true,*
> *Granny is our name for you."*

"That's not the name my grandson told me," said Granny, and off she went.

Granny's search for an answer took her across the field, over the rocks, through the pasture. She asked the same question of all the animals she met along the way. Donkey bawled, "Haw, hee-haw." Goat bleated, "Bleah, bleah-bleah." Cow answered, "Moo, moo-moo." None of that would do.

At last Granny came to the beach. Turtle was sunning himself on the sand, out of reach of the waves. She sat down beside him and asked:

> *"Turtle, did you teach my name?*
> *My grandson says it well.*
> *Were you the one who made him promise*
> *Not to tell?"*

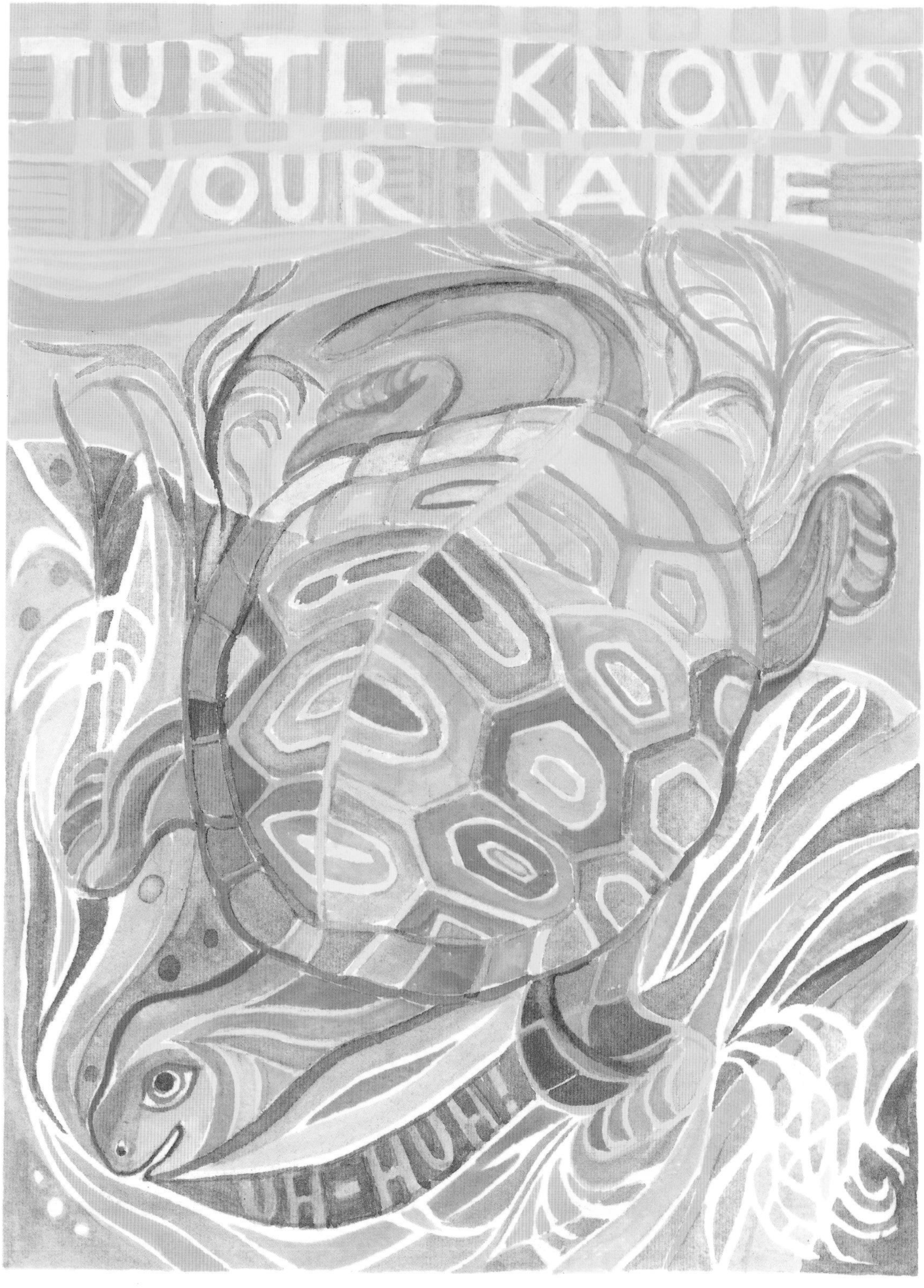
TURTLE KNOWS
YOUR NAME
UH-HUH!

Turtle answered:

"Yes, I taught your grandson
To say your name.
I thought it was the thing to do.
And now, I'll tell it to you, too.
It's MAPASEEDO JACKALINDY EYE PIE TACKARINDY."

Granny leaped up and spun with the news.
"How did you remember my long, long name from so long ago?"
asked Granny.
Turtle answered:

"I learn names from the beach name dances.
I remember them well, because I take no chances.
I swim up and listen, though you don't see me.
Then I spell your names in shells at the bottom of the sea."

Turtle rose up on his short legs and waddled to the water. With a
swish, swoosh, he slipped into the sea.
Granny waved as Turtle swam out. He dove and disappeared as
Granny sang:

"Turtle knows your name, uh-huh!
Turtle knows your name."

When Granny reached home, her grandson stood at the door with an empty plate. He'd eaten all the bread pudding.

"Oh, MAPASEEDO JACKALINDY EYE PIE TACKARINDY," he said, "now for some sweet-potato pie."

"Aha, UPSILIMANA TUMPALERADO," said MAPASEEDO JACKALINDY EYE PIE TACKARINDY, "I know who knows our names."

They smiled at each other and called out together:

"Turtle knows your name!"

Then MAPASEEDO JACKALINDY EYE PIE TACKARINDY hugged UPSILIMANA TUMPALERADO and cut two slices of sweet-potato pie.

"Thank you, MAPASEEDO JACKALINDY EYE PIE TACKARINDY," said UPSILIMANA TUMPALERADO. "I love your pudding. I love your sweet-potato pie."

"Well, good, UPSILIMANA TUMPALERADO," said MAPASEEDO JACKALINDY EYE PIE TACKARINDY. "You can thank Turtle for dessert."

"Uh-huh, MAPASEEDO JACKA…"

But before he could finish saying her name, Granny clapped her hand over her grandson's mouth.

"Listen," she said, "promise not to tell anyone else my name. And from now on, just call me 'Granny' and nothing more. Call me 'Granny,' the way you did before."

UPSILIMANA TUMPALERADO shook his head, and Granny took her hand from his mouth.

"Uh-huh, Granny!" he said.

"And furthermore," said Granny, "from now on, I'm going to call you 'Son.' "

They burst out laughing and finished the pie.

"Mmm...I love you, Granny!"

"Mmmm...mmm...I love you, Son!"

First Aladdin Books edition 1993

Copyright © 1989 by Ashley Bryan

All rights reserved. No part of this book may be reproduced or transmitted in any form or by any means, electronic or mechanical, including photocopying, recording, or by any information storage and retrieval system, without permission in writing from the Publisher.

Aladdin Books
Macmillan Publishing Company
866 Third Avenue
New York, NY 10022

Maxwell Macmillan Canada, Inc.
1200 Eglinton Avenue East
Suite 200
Don Mills, Ontario M3C 3N1

Macmillan Publishing Company is part of the Maxwell Communication Group of Companies.

Printed in Hong Kong

10 9 8 7 6 5 4 3 2 1

A hardcover edition of Turtle Knows Your Name is available from Atheneum, Macmillan Publishing Company.

Library of Congress Cataloging-in-Publication Data
Bryan, Ashley.
Turtle knows your name / retold and illustrated by Ashley Bryan — 1st Aladdin Books ed.
p.   cm.
Summary: A small boy with a very long name is challenged by his grandmother to find out her real name.
ISBN 0-689-71728-8
[1. Folklore — West Indies.]   I. Title.
[PZ8.1.B838Tu   1993]
398.24′52792 — dc20
[E]   92-33553